At The Café Splendid

Terry Denton

For Eve

Houghton Mifflin Company
Boston 1988

Every Friday Adele and her little brother Victor go with their mother to the Café Splendid for afternoon tea.

Adele and Victor love going to the Café Splendid. All the waiters know their names. It is always warm inside in winter and cool in summer.

Victor often talks with the chef in the kitchen.

Adele likes to sit up at the table drinking her favourite lime milkshake.

This Friday is special because it is Adele's birthday. As a treat, she has been given permission to perform her magic show. Adele has been practising for weeks. Victor will be her assistant.

Adele and Victor get ready near the piano. Adele is a little nervous because so many people will be watching.

Suddenly, Victor is gone!

And with him the magic wand, top hat, cape, and all the tricks!

Adele chases Victor over
the chairs and under the
tables and into the kitchen.

The chef helps Adele search for Victor. She hears a crash as Victor races out the door.

The three white doves escape
and fly cooing into the air.

Victor runs off again with
Adele close behind.

A snaky trail of silk leads off into the cloakroom. It took Adele ages to tie those scarves together.

Adele looks for Victor among
the heavy winter coats and the
hats with fruit on top.

The top hat hops towards her. Could this be Victor? No, it is Roger, the pet rabbit, who gives a startled squeak.

Adele then hears a loud sneeze from behind the piano.

She sees her magic pack of cards fly up into the
air.

Adele chases Victor round and round the restaurant.

Where has that Victor gone?

A thousand flowers burst from the magic wand. Now all Adele's tricks are ruined!

Victor makes a final dash
for the table.

Suddenly the lights go out in the Café Splendid.

When they come up again, there on the table is the biggest birthday cake Adele has ever seen.

Everyone shouts surprise and sings Happy Birthday.

Adele is very surprised but also sad because she can't perform her magic show.

But then Adele remembers just
one more trick. She takes one of
the marzipan eggs from the top of
the birthday cake.

With a flourish of her scarlet silk scarf
and the magic words Splendid
Strawberry Cream Cake, the egg
disappears.

And then reappears.

Everyone applauds and shouts hooray, even Victor. Adele's magic show is a grand success.

Adele, Victor, their mother,
Roger the rabbit and the three
doves proceed home in the cold
night air. It's been the most
wonderful birthday after all, but
now it's time for bed.

Library of Congress Cataloging-in-Publication Data

Denton, Terry.
　At the Café Splendid.

　Summary: Adele plans a magic show for her
birthday celebration at the Café Splendid, but
her little brother almost ruins her plans.
　[1. Birthdays — Fiction. 2. Restaurants,
lunch rooms, etc. — Fiction] I. Title.
PZ7.D4374At　1988　　[E]　　87-16957
ISBN 0-395-46476-5

Printed in Hong Kong

10 9 8 7 6 5 4 3 2 1

*The Author would like to thank Rita Scharf of Oxford University
Press for the idea of the Café Splendid and her assistance in
developing the book.*